Splat the Cat
Back to School, Splat!

Based on the bestselling books by Rob Scotton
Cover art by Rob Scotton
Text by Laura Bergen
Interior Pencils by Charles Grosvenor • Interior Color by Joe Merkel

HARPER FESTIVAL
An Imprint of HarperCollinsPublishers

For Marley. Let your imagination guide you. —R.S.

HarperFestival is an imprint of HarperCollins Publishers.
Splat the Cat: Back to School, Splat!
Copyright © 2011 by Rob Scotton
All rights reserved. Manufactured in China.
No part of this book may be used or reproduced in any manner whatsoever without written permission
except in the case of brief quotations embodied in critical articles and reviews. For information address
HarperCollins Children's Books, a division of HarperCollins Publishers, 10 East 53rd Street, New York, NY 10022.
www.harpercollinschildrens.com
Library of Congress catalog number: 2010942559
ISBN 978-0-06-197851-7
Typography by Rick Farley
11 12 13 14 15 SCP 10 9 8 7 6 5 4 3 2
❖
First Edition

Splat's tail wiggled wildly with excitement as he walked to Cat School. It was the first day of a new school year, and he could not wait to see his old friends and his teacher, Mrs. Wimpydimple.

Splat's tail dragged behind him as he walked home that afternoon.
Now he was not excited at all.

It was the end of the first day of a new school year, and he already
had homework!

"What's wrong, Splat?" asked his little sister.

"I have to do a show-and-tell about my summer vacation," Splat said.

"That sounds like fun," said his little sister.

"But I did so many super things. How can I choose just one thing to show?" Splat said.

Over the summer Splat rode his bike in a very important race.

"Can I come, too?" asked Splat's little sister.
"Little sisters' bikes are not fast enough to race," Splat said.

But she tagged along anyway.

And he went swimming with sharks in the ocean.

"Can I come, too?" asked Splat's little sister.
"Little sisters aren't strong enough to fight off sharks," Splat said.

But she tagged along anyway.

Splat also played in a big soccer game.

"Can I come, too?" asked Splat's little sister.
"Little sisters aren't big enough to play soccer," Splat said.

But she tagged along anyway.

Splat went searching for pirate treasure.

"Can I come, too?" asked Splat's little sister.
"Finding treasure is too hard for little sisters," Splat said.

But she tagged along anyway.

Splat even built a rocket ship to launch him into space.

"Can I come, too?" asked Splat's little sister.
"Not now!" Splat said. "I'm counting. Ten . . . Nine . . .
Eight . . . Seven . . . Six . . . Five . . . uh-oh . . . I forget what comes next. . . ."

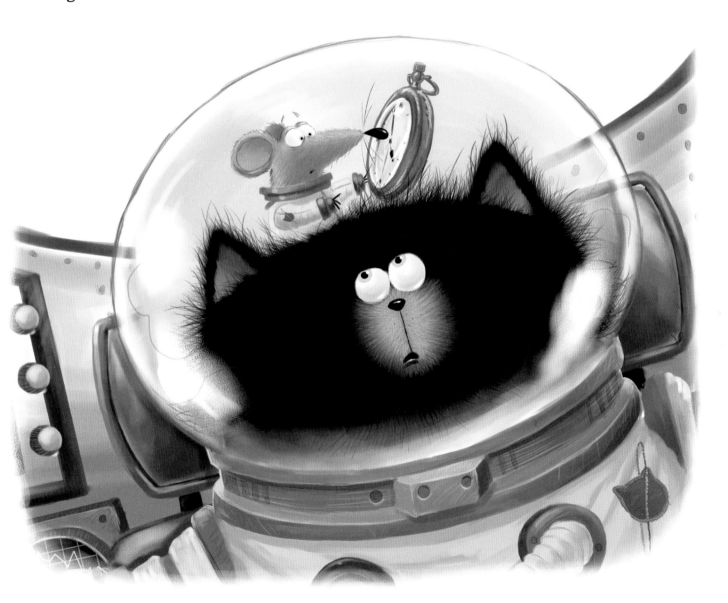

She tagged along anyway.
". . . Four, Three, Two, One, Blastoff!" she said.

"I had lots of adventures," Splat told Seymour. "How can I possibly choose just one thing to show?"

Seymour shrugged. He didn't have any ideas.

Suddenly Splat thought of something.
There *was* one really important thing he could show!

The next day, Splat went to school with his tail wiggling wildly.
And Splat was most pleased that his sister tagged along, too!